To Molly, for turning a wish into a star.
To Maria, for believing.
And to starkeepers everywhere.

All rights reserved. Published in the United States by Random House Children's Books,
a division of Penguin Random House LLC, New York.

Random House and the colophon are registered trademarks of Penguin Random House LLC.

Visit us on the Web! rhcbooks.com

Educators and librarians, for a variety of teaching tools, visit us at RHTeachersLibrarians.com

Library of Congress Cataloging-in-Publication Data
Name: Pray, Faith, author, illustrator.
Title: The starkeeper / written and illustrated by Faith Pray.
Description: First edition. | New York : Random House Children's Books, [2020] |
Audience: Ages 3–7. | Audience: Grades K–1. |
Summary: In a dark, rainy, lonely world a girl's wish brings a star to earth,
but its light fades until her acts of kindness make the star spark and flame.
Identifiers: LCCN 2019028906 (print) | LCCN 2019028907 (ebook) |
ISBN 978-1-9848-9270-6 (hardcover) | ISBN 978-1-9848-9271-3 (library binding) |
ISBN 978-1-9848-9272-0 (ebook)
Subjects: CYAC: Stars—Fiction. | Kindness—Fiction.
Classification: LCC PZ7.1.P6993 St 2020 (print) | LCC PZ7.1.P6993 (ebook) | DDC [E]—dc23

MANUFACTURED IN CHINA
10 9 8 7 6 5 4 3 2 1
First Edition

The starkeeper

written and illustrated by

Faith Pray

Random House 🏠 New York

The world had been dark for a long time.
Rainy. Lonely. Dark.

Every morning, the girl fed the fish and waited
for things to be different.

But every morning, the world stayed the same.

On one especially wet day, the girl got tired
of waiting.

She made an enormous wish. She wished the
lonely dark away.

A star!

It was beautiful and warm and perfect.
She longed to keep it for herself.

But the girl could tell that the star didn't want to be kept hidden. It needed the girl to help it shine.

Surely the best place for a star to light up the world, she thought, was someplace grand.

But the people in the fancy house were busy. They didn't even want to stop and see the star.

The girl and the star felt small.

Next, the girl tried taking it to the shops.
Shopkeepers are sensible, the girl figured.
Maybe they would know what to do.

But even though she
knocked and knocked,
the doors stayed shut.

The girl and the star shivered.

Finally, the girl took the star to the center of the village.
Maybe someone there would be able to help.

But no one seemed interested.

The star was gloomy now.
Shrinkier. Wilted. The girl
felt it, too. By now, the star
was as small as a smudge.
And the world felt the same.

I must not be very good at taking care of stars,
thought the girl. *Perhaps I should forget my wish.*
Someone else could try to help it shine.
She found a perfect spot for giving up.

Only, someone was already there.
Two someones.

Maybe there *was* something the girl could do.

It was a very small thing.

She shared her sweater . . . and a tiny piece of the star.

Now the star seemed rounder. Shinier. Glowy.

Maybe, thought the girl, there
were lots of small somethings
she could do with the star.

The girl and the star went everywhere.
Each time she found something to do
or someone to help, the girl broke off
a bit of the star.

And each time, the star grew.

Maybe she did know
how to be a starkeeper.

Because it did shine.
Not all at once.
Not in a grand way.
But in tiny sparks that
warmed and flamed . . .

. . . and joined stars upon
stars upon stars
that chased away
the lonely dark.

And the world was different.

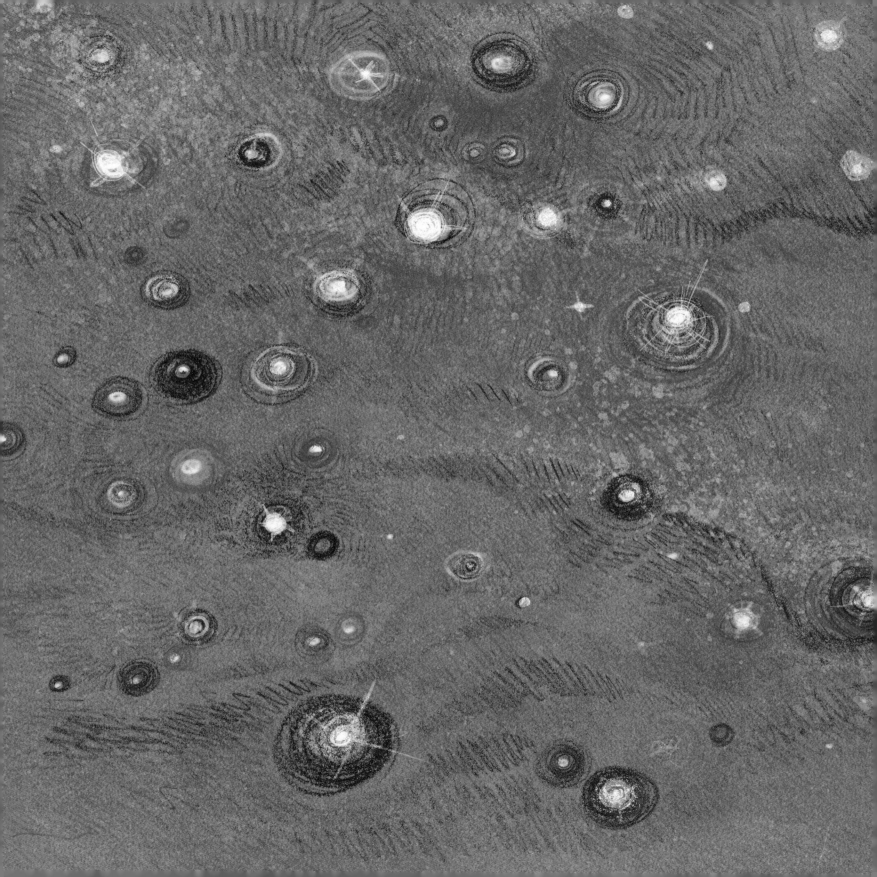